Twee Tale

Collected Sho
by Diane Wordsworth
Volume 2

Baggins Bottom Books

Also by Diane Wordsworth

Marcie Craig mysteries
Night Crawler

Tarot Tales
The Ace of Wands
The Ace of Cups

Toni & Bart time-travel tales
Mardi Gras

Wordsworth Collections
Twee Tales
Twee Tales Too
Twee Tales Twee
Flash Fiction: Five Very Short Stories

Words Worth Reading

Issue 1: October 2021

Wordsworth Shorts
The Spirit of the Wind
The Most Scariest Night of the Year
The Girl on the Bench
Dancing on Ice
Happy Christmas, Santa
Careful What You Wish For
New Year's Revolution
One Born Every Minute
The Mystery of Woolley Dam
Martha's Favourite Doll
The Complete Angler

Wordsworth Writers' Guides
Diary of a Scaredy Cat
Project Management for Writers: Gate 1 – What?

Watch for more at https://dianewordsworth.com.

Table of Contents

Spring 1

Around the Maypole 3

Going, Going, Gone 9

Alexandra's Ragtag Band 17

Summer 23

It Wasn't Me 25

Meet Me in Glenridding 31

The Battle of Killiecrankie 35

The Complete Angler 41

After the Storm 47

Autumn 53

Emma 55

Trick or Treat 57

Burn 63

Winter 69

Don't Break a Leg 71

Breaking the Ice 79

Dancing on Ice 85

About the author 89

Catch up with Diane today 91

Also by Diane Wordsworth 93

For Ian, always

Spring

AROUND THE MAYPOLE, first published in *Twee Tales Too*
GOING, GOING, GONE, first published in *Woman's Era* in India,
by Diane Parkin
ALEXANDRA'S RAGTAG BAND, first published in *My Weekly*, by
Diane Parkin

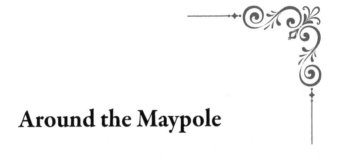

Around the Maypole

CLAIRE WATCHED ALL of the other children dancing around the maypole with envy. May Day was, traditionally, the start of the summer festivities in the village and everyone looked forward to the day throughout the winter months. The ancient pagan rituals were given the nod in the old fertility celebrations but, of course, the children didn't understand any of that. Even some of the adults didn't know any of that. They just enjoyed the fun, the fair, the dancing and the holiday atmosphere. The only reason Claire knew much of the history was because her parents were on the village committee and so arranged a lot of the historical jollies.

"Doesn't your sister look lovely?" said Claire's mum.

Claire looked as far sideways as the horrid neck brace would let her and agreed. Kitty did indeed look beautiful in her May Queen splendour, while at the same time looking awkward and embarrassed in her crown made from pretty spring flowers.

"She looks as though she's hating every second," laughed Claire. Then she painfully and slowly returned her glance towards the dancers, who were skipping in and out in time to the music, twisting the colourful ribbons around the pole under her sister's regal gaze.

Kitty's first handmaiden Ellie looked as though she would burst into tears at any moment while the page boy, Thomas, was far more engrossed with something he couldn't quite reach up his nose. Most of the other handmaidens watched the dancing, waiting until it would be their turn.

Claire would normally be dancing too, now with the older girls or later looking after the little ones. Many thought that she preferred to dance so that she didn't have to go through the humiliation of the annual beauty contest. But really, she just loved to dance. She was too old to be May Queen now anyway and, personally, couldn't understand those parents that forced their daughters to compete, or why any of the other girls would want to anyway. It just wasn't her thing, but dancing was. Claire's parents, fortunately, had always let their girls make up their own minds about what they wanted to do, despite being on the committee. And Kitty was secretly delighted to have been chosen this year – she just didn't want to seem uncool to her friends.

At the moment, though, Claire was still learning how to walk again, or constantly hiding the neck brace they made her wear today – for her own good, apparently. She hated the thing, she hated the wheelchair she was gradually learning to do without, and she hated not being able to join in with the dancing. But more than that, much more than any of that, she hated the reckless car driver who had put her in the stupid wheelchair in the first place.

Claire's dad had complained quite aggressively about the man being drunk, and how three months in prison wasn't anywhere near sufficient punishment for ruining his oldest daughter's dream.

Claire had already graduated onto her blocks and had been picked to play Clara in her dance company's Christmas production of *The Nutcracker Suite* – every girl ballerina's dream, that or the Sugar Plum Fairy. Instead she'd woken up in a hospital bed two weeks later with no recollection of the accident. Her mum had said that was a blessing, but still the psychotherapist probed, trying to bring back her memory. Claire didn't care if they never did. One minute she was due to perform the role of her life (so far), and the next minute it was all over with no firm chance of her even walking again, let alone dancing. And her vile enemy Nessa 'Grotbag' Pound performed the role instead. Evil witch.

Claire was gutted and, as is the tendency of an already angst-ridden tormented fourteen-year-old, her life was over.

A ROUND OF APPLAUSE broke out as the older girls finished their dance, and mayhem erupted as all of the younger children scrambled for their go or wailed because they couldn't have the coloured ribbon they wanted. Once upon a time the ribbons would be unwound and used again. But these days, to save time – and yet more aggravation while the little ones impatiently waited – they used another layer of ribbons.

"I got you some candyfloss," said a voice at her side, distracting her again, and a massive pink and blue bundle of froth appeared in front of her.

"Thanks," she grinned, taking the stick. Damien was her best friend and always seemed to know what she would like and when.

"Well, you won't be watching your weight at the moment –" Claire punched him on the thigh. "Woo, and your strength's coming back."

"I need to watch my weight even more for as long as I'm stuck in this thing," she joked. But she enjoyed the sugary mess anyway, and tried not to worry too much when it got stuck all over her nose and in her hair.

"Who's last up?" asked Damien as they watched the young children getting all tangled up to the music and finding it hilariously funny.

"Handmaidens and pages are last," she said, nodding towards her sister, who was so bored by now that she was gazing at the sky.

"Bet you can't wait until you can join them again."

"I'm joining them already. We're up next."

CLAIRE HAD INITIALLY reacted very badly to the accident. But during the short months of operations, convalescence and physiotherapy, she'd got chatting to some of the other youngsters in wheelchairs. Youngsters who would always be in wheelchairs but who still filled their busy lives with all sorts of interests and activities, some that even many able-bodied kids would never have the chance to try, or who would forever be too lazy. And it was while watching highlights from the Olympics and Paralympics that the germ of an idea had formed in her mind. She put it to her parents, who in turn put it to the village committee.

"COME ON," SAID CLAIRE to Damien, discarding her sticky candyfloss stick in a litter bin that was close by. "You can push me."

Damien did as he was told, not knowing what Claire had in mind.

Because her injuries were healing, and because she was gradually walking more and more, Claire no longer qualified for a battery-operated wheelchair, and her arms were developing rather too well for a dainty prima ballerina's. She'd have to lose those muscles before she started dancing again – no one wanted to see a ballerina with bigger biceps than Arnold Schwarzenegger. So while Damien was around, she may as well make good use of him.

The little ones had been untangled now and all of the ribbons straightened, and there was an extra announcement while they changed the music and the next group of dancers found their places.

"As you know," said Claire's dad over the PA, "Claire, older sister of this year's May Queen and our other daughter, was involved in a serious road accident." He waited as a sympathetic murmur rippled through the crowd. "But like the rest of us she's bouncing back and this year suggested an addition to our dances around the maypole."

There was a flurry of activity around the maypole and another buzz of applause from the audience. Damien pushed Claire into place and started to leave.

"You're not going anywhere," she hissed, and the colour drained from his face as he realised what she was suggesting...

"You w-want m-me to d-dance?"

"Dance with me," she grinned, taking hold of her ribbon.

The music started and a collection of Claire's friends from the hospital, in wheelchairs or on crutches, moved in time to the slightly slower music.

The less-abled maypole dance was a huge success and everyone agreed that they should do it again next year. But next year Claire fully intended to be back on her own two feet and dancing with the able-bodied older girls again – or maybe they could integrate the two.

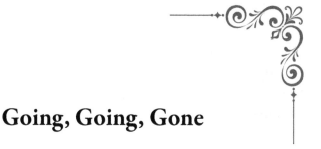

Going, Going, Gone

THERE WAS NO DOUBT about it. The music box Grandad had brought back from Italy after the war was hideous. It looked like Walt Disney's castle, in a gaudy way, and was allegedly part of a pair. But it was tasteless and tacky and now it was gone. Instead of feeling elation, though, Abigail was distraught.

"I have to find it," she told her friend.

"But it sounds vile," said Laura. "You should be grateful the house clearance people took it. They normally leave tat like that behind." She took a sip from her Archers. "Where's the problem?"

"It was Grandad's music box," wailed Abigail, glugging her own Bacardi Breezer.

"I thought you said he died ages ago."

"He did. But his ashes are in it."

For as long as Abigail could remember the dreaded music box had taken pride of place on Granny's mantelpiece. She had never heard a single note, due mainly to the contents, but also because Granny kept it well and truly locked.

Granny often spoke of the day she'd be reunited with her husband. Abigail had yet to find a man who would instil in her that kind of loyalty. But she lived in hope. And to keep her in on the pact, Granny had given Abigail the key, making her swear to do her bidding. She'd simply forgot to mention what, precisely, that bidding was.

Now Granny had gone... but so had Grandad's ashes.

"I have to bring it back," declared Abigail, determined. She had no idea where to start, but now the decision had been made she was able to move on. "Not a word to Mum," she warned. "The less she knows about this, the better. She'd be mortified if she knew what had happened. She's the one who arranged the house clearance before she and Dad went to the seaside."

THE HOUSE CLEARANCE people were easy enough to find, but once Abigail described the item, her spirits dropped again.

"Sorry, duck," said the old man, pushing his cap to the back of his head. "That music box was so 'orrible we didn't think anyone would want to buy it."

"What did you do with it?"

He scratched his head, then repositioned the cap so the peak came down over his eyebrows. "I think 'e put it in for the auction. That's next week. In Warwickshire, I think. It'll already be there, no doubt. Or on its way. They like 'em a week or so in advance so's the punters can examine the goods, like."

"Do you have the address?" asked Abigail, scrabbling in her bag for a pen and paper.

"Nah. But it'll be on the Internet. I can give you a website address."

Abigail made a note of the URL and found everything she needed to know on the website. It wasn't too far away, in a little place called Knowle, which wasn't in Warwickshire anymore in any case. She could take a couple of days off work and drive over there.

WHEN IT STARTS TO RAIN in England it forgets to stop. It was banging down on the street outside the tiny auction room, which was probably rarely stuffed with so many people.

Abigail had never been to an auction before. "What if I run out of money?" she asked Laura. "It's probably worth thirty quid, but I'll only have about a hundred on me."

"Just shake your head. Make it clear you've gone as high as you can. But if it's only worth thirty pounds, you should be fine."

Now, as rain hammered down outside, Abigail played with the tiny key she'd hung on a chain around her neck. "Look after that," Granny had said. "It's very precious. I'll need it if I'm to be reunited with your grandad."

The music box was lot 144. She'd already been and looked at it about a hundred times, but she went to have another look. The lots were displayed around the room on plinths with numbers on them to match the lot numbers. A little man in a brown overall scuttled to and fro whenever a lot was due. They were currently on number 36. There was ages yet so she felt quite safe sneaking in another peek.

Oh no! Who was that? Someone was looking at her music box. He was tall with dark messy hair that was cut short in some attempt to tame it. But the rain had caused it to curl and stand up about his ears. He looked quite cute... what was she doing? This man was handling her music box, turning it upside down. Poor Grandad! Why? He couldn't possibly like it. It was grotesque.

Abigail kept her eye on the tall stranger who, while he did have a bit of a browse, kept returning to her music box. The house clearance man had told her no one would be interested in the horrid thing. So who was this?

WHEN LOT 143 WAS CALLED, Abigail made her way back to the action. The brown-clad man had moved her music box closer to the podium. She was frustrated to see that the tall stranger was suddenly interested too. Hopefully he'd be her only competition. But even that was too much.

The bidding started at just £10, alternating between Abigail and the man. He kept bettering her by five pounds, so she did the same. When they got to £50, it started jumping up by £10 a time. How did that happen? Neither of them had said anything. Abigail didn't even wave her stick with the number on anymore. The auctioneer knew it was just between the two of them.

Seventy pounds now, and Abigail's turn. She nodded. Eighty. He nodded. Ninety. She nodded. A hundred. That was her limit. He nodded. Abigail hated him. One hundred and ten. She hesitated. There was always her petrol money. Abigail nodded. One hundred and twenty. He didn't even pause, just nodded straight away. One hundred and thirty.

She had just one more fiver.

"Your bid," said the auctioneer.

Abigail took a deep breath and held up her hand showing all five fingers. Her heart was racing. This was her maximum.

"One thirty-five," said the auctioneer. The man nodded. "One forty." He looked at Abigail. "Your bid, madam."

She burst into tears and dashed out into the rain. She didn't even hear the auctioneer's 'going, going, gone', but she knew he must have said it. All she could actually hear was a rushing through her head. It turned out to be traffic swooshing by on the wet road.

Through tear-filled eyes and the heavy curtain of rain, she watched until she saw a break in the steady stream of cars. Then she ran across the road, head down, and into the small church that was almost opposite. She plonked herself down a few pews from the back and sobbed her heart out. Grandad was lost to her now. And Granny.

"Oh Gran," she whispered. "I've let you down so badly." Then she cried until all of her grief was spent.

"Here," said a deep American voice from the pew behind. She glanced over her shoulder to see a folded man's white handkerchief being passed to her. She held up her tissue to show that she was fine, thanks. But seeing how sodden and useless it was, she smiled weakly and took the hanky.

"Thanks." She dabbed carefully at her nose, not wanting to spoil the pristine cloth. She kept her face down thinking she must look a fright.

"Oh, give it a good old blow," said the American. She did so, making a honking great noise, and started to hand it back to him. As it squelched in her hand, she changed her mind.

"I'll wash it for you," she said.

"Sure," said the American, standing up and making his way to her side. He held out a hand. "The name's Toby Vincenzo –"

"Oh," she said, flatly, fighting the fury as she saw his face. "It's you."

"Gee, I'm sorry, Miss...?" She didn't fill him in. "Well, I didn't think it was something worth crying over," he said. "It's only an old musical box. Not a very nice one at that. And the key's missing –"

"Only a musical box?" she spat, shuffling along the wooden seat. "It's only my grandad in there. That's all. It contains his ashes." The American's face froze. That changed his tune. She reached inside her shirt and waved the chain at him. "Here's the key."

Toby tried to hide a smirk that was tugging at his lips. "I'm glad you find it so funny," said Abigail, shivering. "I've taken a day off work and followed that music box halfway across the county to have it snatched from under my nose. And it's hideous, as you've just said, so why do you want it?"

The American's face sobered again. "I've followed that musical box halfway across the world," he said, calmly. "It's cost me a lot of money and I've taken a month off work. It might be hideous, but my own grandfather made it before he emigrated to the States. It's one of a pair. Yours is Cinderella's Castle, my grandma's is Sleeping Beauty's. She wanted this one to make the set after I saw it on the Internet. I had a bit of a rush to get here in time. My grandfather passed away last year, but it would have been their seventieth wedding anniversary next month."

"Oh." Abigail felt churlish.

He sat down beside her and she shivered again, so he removed his jacket and draped it across her shoulders. The jacket felt warm and comfortable and had a nice, friendly smell about it.

"You weren't to know," he said. "Just like I didn't know your grandpop's remains were in there." He paused. "Why was it in the sale?"

Abigail poured out the whole story, drawing comfort from Toby's jacket and closeness. When she'd finished, he said: "Shall we go and liberate him?" Abigail nodded and the two of them slipped out of the church and back into the auction room. "You do the honours," he said.

Abigail slid the key into the lock and clicked it once to the side. The box opened to the sound of Strauss, and a little drawer popped out at the bottom too.

It was empty. Spotless. Abigail was stunned. She felt all of the fight leave her body. The entire episode had been a complete waste of time – and of Toby's money. Grandad was gone.

"DON'T FORGET TO DROP by before you leave England," she said to him after a cup of coffee. She was still coming to terms with her disappointment but there was nothing either of them could do. "I have to let you have your handkerchief back."

"I'VE GOT SOME REALLY bad news," Abigail said to her mother the following day. "Let's have a nice cup of tea."

Out came the whole story once again, but instead of being angry or upset, Abigail's mother smiled sympathetically.

"Oh, Abby. Your grandad's already safe. What did you think me and your dad were doing at the seaside? Mum got a bit forgetful after he died and got steadily worse, but I already knew the plan for the ashes to be scattered together where they honeymooned. I cleaned out that ghastly music box and practically paid those people to take it away."

"But the key..."

"I forgot to give it to them." She got up from the table and walked across to the kitchen drawer, fishing a tiny key from the cutlery tray. "Your gran gave me a key too. Perhaps when your lovely American gets here, you can pass it on."

She also fished out a little burgundy box. "This was supposed to be for you on your twenty-fifth birthday."

Abigail took the box from her mother and opened it. Inside, on a bed of blue velvet, lay the most perfect locket, oval in shape with the name 'Abigail' etched onto the face. Abby opened the locket to find a picture of her grandparents on one side, and another of the three of them when she was a very young child on the other. And nestling between were two curly locks of hair, tied together with ribbon.

"Dad's ashes weren't the only thing Mum kept in that box. She kept this safe in the little drawer.

"Oh, Mum. It's terrific."

Just then the doorbell rang and Abigail went to greet an armful of red roses. The message on the card said:

'See you at the weekend, Toby xxx'.

Alexandra's Ragtag Band

TOBY THE BLACK LABRADOR was easy to see in his hi-vis bright yellow harness and jacket. So that he wasn't mistaken for a guide dog for the blind, the word POLICE was emblazoned across the back of the dog coat in silver-grey luminous capital letters. Many passengers using the railway station still wanted to pet and stroke him. It was easy to forget that he was actually working and he carried out his duties admirably on that Friday evening at King's Cross Station in London.

Toby had been trained to sniff out drugs and explosives and was part of a four-man (or woman) two-dog team.

THE SEVEN MEMBERS OF Alexandra's Ragtag Band lounged untidily amongst their luggage and their instruments on the cold, tiled station floor. Normally they'd be busking or jamming in such a busy environment, but today they were tired and all jammed out. They'd been away for four days, had worked for most of that time, and they'd had a long journey home on the Harwich boat train – and they still weren't home yet.

They'd had a great time entertaining the passengers in the restaurant car or ambling along to the music through the carriages, and that was how they'd earned their passage. On the ferry too.

The band competition they'd taken part in, in Haarlem, had been fantastic. They'd done a good job coming fifth out of so many entrants. No prize money this time but a lot of fun and some good exposure for them. They'd already been booked to go back in the summer and another venue was contacting them in the next few days.

But now the trip was catching up on them and they were tired.

"Uh-oh," warned Alex, after whom the band was named. "Here come the sniffer police." She wasn't really called Alexandra, just plain old Alex, but nobody checked. She played the trumpet.

"And it looks as though he's coming this way," agreed Manjit, the only other female of the group. She played banjo.

"Who's got it this time?" hissed Brian, the unlikely but Mohican punk who played snare drum.

"I do," replied Leon the hippy. He played the tuba.

With Jonah the giant Jamaican on big bass drum, Neil the wannabe gigolo on slide trombone, and Arabian Imran on, rather surprisingly, piano-accordion, they really did make a motley crew. But as that band name was already taken, of a fashion, the raggle-taggle band of oddballs had instead decided on a parody of Irving Berlin's *Alexander's Ragtime Band*. The new name suited them and they had all, in fact, been born and bred in England – apart from gigolo Neil who was born in Scotland but brought up in England.

"Don't look him in the eye," said Alex quietly, and they all instead began to rummage through their luggage. But it was too late. Toby the black labrador sniffer dog with POLICE emblazoned across his back homed straight in on Leon the hippy's hard tuba case.

Leon went quietly, glancing quickly at the others. He knew they'd be waiting for him when he came back.

THE ROOM THEY TOOK him to was white and cold and clinical. The police tried to look disinterested while the station security staff tried to look fierce. There were two of each and Toby, who received a biscuit and a quick chuck behind the ears as he sat patiently and thumped his tail on the floor.

While the male security officer checked his passport and asked the questions, the female security officer emptied the contents of the tuba case onto a table and examined each item one-by-one. She wasn't interested in his other luggage because Toby hadn't been interested either, which was just as well as it was mostly dirty laundry.

And so the perfunctory staccato questioning began. Leon tried not to sound too rehearsed but made sure to give more information than less in his replies to speed things along a bit.

"Where are you travelling today, Mister... uh..." he checked the name on the passport.

"Leon. It's Leon," said Leon. "I'm on my way home."

"Where is home?"

"We're waiting for the connection to Doncaster. The last one was cancelled and the next one's running late."

"Where have you been?"

Leon resisted pointing out that the security guard had all of his travel itinerary along with his passport. "Haarlem. In Holland."

"What was your business in the Netherlands?"

Leon glanced across at his tuba that the female security guard was patiently dismantling where she could, but he resisted... "We were in a band competition."

"How did you get from Haarlem to King's Cross?"

"We came via Amsterdam and the Hook of Holland and caught the boat train from Harwich."

"Surely it would be easier to fly from Schiphol to Doncaster?"

"No, they decided not to fly that route from Robin Hood Airport in the end. We'd have to come in to Humberside or Manchester instead."

"But that would still be quicker than coming through London."

"Yes, but it's cheaper by train and we work our passage. That way it costs us nothing in the end, and we get paid."

"How did you do in the competition?"

"We came fifth. Out of forty-five."

The security guard raised an eyebrow and looked impressed for a moment. But he seemed to be all out of questions and the female security guard seemed to have exhausted all avenues with the tuba case. Leon tried not to get annoyed that someone else had mauled his instrument, but he knew it would be covered with fingerprints by now.

The security guard turned towards the security guardette. "What did you find?"

"Nothing," she said, indicating the table in front of her. Even the x-ray machine had remained idle. The tuba was in as many pieces as it broke down to for cleaning purposes, she'd opened a small bottle of Brasso, a green cleaning cloth covered with smudges lay spread out next to the Brasso, a pair of ladies gardening gloves (pink, flowery) were next to that, and there were a few mini sheets of music.

"There must be something," said Mister Security, but Miss Security simply shrugged her shoulders and shook her head.

There was nothing.

Mister Security looked across to Toby's handler. "Can the dog come and identify what it was he could smell?"

The policeman nodded and fetched Toby to the table. Toby panted happily, wagged his tail twice, and woofed quietly at the gloves.

"Thank you," said the security man, and Toby and his handler resumed their place alongside the policewoman. Toby received another treat.

"Can you tell me, Mister... uh..." said the security guard.

"Leon," reminded Leon, helpfully.

"Er... yes, why do you have a pair of gardening gloves in your case?"

"They're for when I'm polishing the brass. They save me getting fingerprints everywhere." He glanced pointedly at the security woman, who didn't even have the good grace to blush.

"But these are gardening gloves. Ladies gardening gloves."

"Yes, they're much cheaper than the white polishing gloves and those came free on the front of a gardening magazine."

"Do you also use them for gardening?"

Leon thought for a moment. "Yes, actually... I think I did use those... when I fertilised the grass. The fertiliser grains burn my skin, so I used the gloves when I scattered it."

Tony's handler cleared his throat.

"Yes?" said the security guard.

"What kind of fertiliser do you use, Sir?"

"Bone meal. Fish, blood and bone."

"Ah." The policeman looked at the security guard. "Could we have a word?"

Mister Security smiled unsmilingly as he excused himself and the police officer. When they returned, Miss Security was told to put everything back, Leon was given his passport and travel itinerary, and he was told he could go.

"We're sorry to have detained you, Mister... uh... Sir."

AS EXPECTED THE REST of Leon's band mates were waiting for him.

"All okay?" asked Jonah the giant Jamaican.

"All okay," grinned Leon.

"Come on, then. Our train's on platform seven."

And the unlikely raggle-taggle group of oddballs finally completed the last leg of their journey home.

TWO DAYS LATER, ON Sunday, the band met up again, this time at the bandstand in Rotherham's Rosehill Park. They were fully garbed out in the band's livery of black trousers, black waistcoats with red shiny satin back panels, fluorescent turquoise shiny satin shirts, and sparkly black bowler hats with turquoise and red shiny satin ribbon around the rims.

Alex's hair was already short, but Manjit pinned hers into a neat little bun, Brian hid his Mohican under his hat, and Leon tied his beaded braids into a ponytail.

They were ready to entertain Rotherham on this sunny Sunday afternoon.

"Okay," said Manjit on banjo. "Who has the Dutch beers?"

"Me," said Jonah the giant Jamaican on big bass drum. "Who has the 'cakes'?"

"Me," said Alex on trumpet, after whom the band was named. "Who has the 'smokes'?"

"Me," said Neil the wannabe gigolo on slide trombone.

"And whose turn is it next time to carry the decoy through customs?" asked Leon the hippy on tuba.

"Mine," said Arabian Imran who, rather surprisingly, played piano-accordion.

"Perfect," said Brian the unlikely punk who played snare drum.

"We don't get stopped that often, thankfully," said Alex. "But when we do, that bone meal certainly confuses the dogs."

They all grinned at each other and then Alexandra's Ragtag Band began to tune-up.

Summer

IT WASN'T ME, first published in *Twee Tales Too*
MEET ME IN GLENRIDDING, first published in *Twee Tales Too*
THE BATTLE OF KILLIECRANKIE, first published in *The People's Friend*
THE COMPLETE ANGLER, first published in *The People's Friend*
AFTER THE STORM, first published in *Twee Tales Too*

It Wasn't Me

ZIGGY RAN HIS FINGERS through his hair in frustration. He hadn't planned this first weekend very well at all.

He had the official opening of the new retail premises and all the paraphernalia that went with that, he had his very first commercial commission, and it was his turn to have his six-year-old son Abe as well. As if he didn't have enough to worry about looking after the pathologically clumsy boy, everything was going wrong and Abe wanted to spend his whole time in the new shop – but what child wouldn't want to be surrounded by chocolate? He kept on eating the display and every time his dad caught him, complete with tell-tale chocolate smudges all around his face, the little boy would declare, in all sincerity: "It wasn't me."

It was Saturday morning. The grand opening ceremony for the shop was 1pm. Ziggy had to get a chocolate fountain and two massive black forest gateaux to the engagement party venue by noon, and set the fountain up so that the happy couple could switch it on when they were ready. He'd also individually wrapped, in red and gold cellophane, sixty hand-made chocolates, pralines, truffles, toffees and so on.

But someone was stealing the favours.

"It wasn't me," assured Abe.

"How about a chocolate hunt?" suggested Ziggy at last, not knowing what else to do.

"Do I get to eat them?"

"Only if you find all of them."

Abraham put on what he thought was a grown-up puzzled face while he weighed the idea up.

"I can count to ten…" he said at last.

"You can count to a hundred, you little tinker. But I'll hide just fifteen of them," he said, wrapping some 'rejects' in blue cellophane. "When you find them all," he reached up to get an empty plastic dish off a shelf, "I want you to put them in here." He put the dish where Abe could reach it. "When you have all fifteen you can eat one –"

"One?" yelled the boy. He was learning some things far too quickly.

"Okay two – but only if you're good and concentrate on the game. And you have to count to a hundred out loud while I hide them. With your eyes shut."

Abraham closed his eyes tight and counted clearly, slowly and loudly while Ziggy hid some chocolates in relatively easy places and some in slightly more difficult ones. He made sure, though, that he could see his son all the time he was working.

IT TOOK HIM SLIGHTLY longer than he hoped, but the two-tier chocolate cake centrepiece for the window display was finally finished, and so were all the things he needed to take to the party.

"You can have a chocolate now," Ziggy said, surprised but quite proud that his son had found all fifteen reasonably quickly. "So long as you didn't peek." Abe shook his head and crossed his heart. "Okay then, you can have another after we've swept up that cocoa powder you spilled."

"It wasn't me," said Abraham.

The six-year-old helped his dad to pack everything for the party very carefully in open-topped cardboard boxes. Ziggy had also obtained some chocolate cosmos flowers to add a finishing flourish – he'd pinched some for his window display too. They locked the shop up and drove the new van the short distance to the assembly rooms. A bar had already been set up so Abraham was placed on a chair a safe distance from anything he could damage, with some chocolates and his Nintendo.

Jacqueline, the fiancée, was there to oversee and supervise everything. The party wasn't due to start until much later in the evening so there was a relaxed atmosphere. Abe sat good as gold, sucking his chocolate in his mouth so that it lasted longer. But he wasn't playing with his games console. He was too busy watching his dad demonstrate the chocolate fountain. Abe was fascinated and kept wandering over so he could stick his finger into the flowing chocolate.

"Abe," said Ziggy, "if you promise not to touch, I'll dip some marshmallows in so you can taste it, but you must let me finish setting up first."

"Okay," said the boy, returning to his seat. And that's how he was the first to see the funny man at the door who wobbled a bit as he came in and kept bumping into chairs, tables, imaginary objects. Ziggy gave the man a wide berth as he went out to get the last of the boxes from the van. The gateaux he was collecting would need to be kept cool until the party later.

Abraham sat quietly on his chair. The party lady smiled at him and ruffled his hair, but she stiffened when she saw the drunk.

"Mark! What are you doing here?"

The funny man was already close enough by now for Abe to smell him, and he carried on to where the chocolate fountain and engagement cake were on display.

"I don't believe you're engaged," he slurred. "It didn't take you very long. Were you seeing him when you were still seeing me?"

"No!" said Jacqueline, horrified. "Oh Mark, please don't spoil things."

"Why not?" He produced a small bottle from his coat pocket and drank noisily from it, although Abe noticed that he dribbled most of it.

"I loved you, Jack," said Mark, lunging towards her. But she jumped out of his way and he stumbled.

OUTSIDE ZIGGY WAS LOCKING the van when he heard the thud, a crash, and then the sound of glass breaking.

"Oh no!" he cried, almost dropping the box as he dashed back inside. What had Abraham done now?

Jacqueline was frozen, a look of shock on her face. The chocolate fountain was in pieces on the floor with liquid chocolate still spurting from the spout and splashing everywhere. A table was on its side, the tablecloth in a crumpled heap on the floor stained with chocolate and with clumps of cake stuck to it. And Abe sat, good as gold on his chair, exactly where Ziggy had left him, eyes wide with surprise, licking the finger he'd used to mop up splashes of chocolate from his clothes.

"I don't need the marshmallows now, Dad –"

Ziggy, a thunderous look on his face, bawled: "ABRAHAM!"

To which the child most truthfully replied: "It wasn't me..."

Ziggy was about to argue when he heard a kerfuffle from behind the upturned table. The drunk was carefully getting back to his feet but he managed to pull what was left of the cake onto the floor and on top of himself.

Jacqueline didn't bother to call the drunk a rude name or to yell at him, but he knew he'd gone too far. He made another attempt to get to his feet, successfully this time, and staggered out of the assembly room with about as much dignity as he could muster.

"Are you all right?" Ziggy asked Jacqueline, himself calmer now. At the same time he checked his son was fine.

"M-m-my c-c-cake," she stammered.

He felt very sorry for her as she started to clean up the mess in a daze. The beautiful two-tier cake was ruined, as was his chocolate fountain, but he could replace that a lot easier than she could the cake.

"Is the lady's party spoiled?" asked Abe sadly.

"It is without the cake," Jacqueline muttered.

Abe tugged at his dad's sleeve and whispered in his ear.

IT WASN'T QUITE WHAT Ziggy had in mind when he planned the grand opening event, but the news story certainly made more of a splash than anyone could have imagined.

Abe and Ziggy had gone back to the shop to replace the fountain with a fondue – he'd have plenty of time to order a new one. The two-tier chocolate cake that took pride of place in the window display was very quickly tarted up with chocolate butter cream, chocolate shavings and a large punnet of fresh raspberries. And the story of how Ziggy had donated his own prized cake to the engaged couple made front page news.

Ziggy couldn't have wished for better publicity, Abe managed not to be sick after eating all of that chocolate, and the happy couple lived happily ever after.

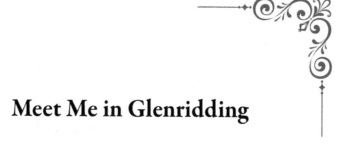

Meet Me in Glenridding

MADDY WAS MORE THAN miffed. Jed had only booked them a holiday and they couldn't afford it. He was out of work and refused point blank to get married until he was earning again. Yet here he was spending part of what should be paying the deposit on a house. They didn't need a holiday. They couldn't afford a holiday.

"It's hardly a holiday," he argued. "It's only down the road for a start–"

"Exactly!" snapped Maddy. "We can go to Ullswater for a day trip any time."

"Ah, but we can't walk up Hallin Fell first thing in the morning and watch the mist rise from the lake. And it's only a B&B, it's hardly the Ritz. Besides, a break will do us good."

Yes, Maddy had to concede, he had a point there. They'd had so much stress since Jed had been laid off. First the house had fallen through, then they'd cancelled the wedding and lost all of the deposits. But they both agreed that the wedding wasn't essential, they'd find another house when they were ready, and so long as they had their health and each other, that was all that mattered. Jed would find a job soon enough... wouldn't he?"

THE FIRST DAY OF THEIR holiday, or 'short break' as Maddy preferred to call it – to ease her conscience – was spent exploring many of the places they already knew so well. They walked up Hallin

Fell after a hairy drive through Martindale and watched the morning mist rise from the lake. They had an orientation drive around the lake, over to Windermere and then back again via Grasmere, where they visited Dove Cottage and ate Rushbearing Gingerbread in the tearoom next door. They even did that tourist thing in Pooley Bridge and fed the ducks and bought ice cream. It was all so civilised and lovely and perfect that Maddy half-expected Jed to propose all over again.

"Are you having a nice time?" Jed asked her over coffee after a very romantic evening meal.

"I'm having a lovely time," she admitted, smiling and holding his hand. And she really was. "It's good to be able to forget everything, just for a day." They hadn't even been bothered by phone calls because there was hardly any signal in Ullswater.

THE FOLLOWING MORNING at eight o'clock they struggled once again through a hearty, freshly cooked, five-course full English breakfast when Jed suddenly jumped to his feet. He dashed down the last of his coffee, grabbed a slice of toast, and kissed Maddy on the top of her head.

"What are you doing?" she asked.

"Here," he said, fishing a ticket out of his wallet and giving it to her. "Meet me in Glenridding at ten o'clock. I'll leave you the car, you can park at the boat station."

"But what about you?"

"I'll see you there. Gotta dash." And he was gone.

Maddy had no idea what he was up to, but he was clearly up to something. There was really nothing more she could do, though, except finish her delicious breakfast.

THE BOAT TICKET JED had given her – another extravagance they could ill-afford – was for the ten o'clock sailing. At a quarter-to she was in the car park paying for her parking ticket and she saw she'd get a free cup of tea over at Pooley Bridge if she kept her stub. Hmm, she thought, tucking it into her purse. Every little helps...

It was another beautiful day without a cloud in the sky. The glass-like surface of Ullswater was navy blue. A lovely day for a steamer ride. Maddy wandered around the souvenir shop, read some of the news stories pasted to the wall, availed herself of the facilities, but there was no sign of Jed.

She made her way down the pier and back, checked the shop in case he'd been in the loo too, looked through the main door towards town to see if he was on his way. No Jed.

The *Raven* chugged her gentle way towards the jetty and, once she was safely tethered, Maddy watched the passengers alight in case Jed was among them. No.

As the boat bounced against the pier and the Glenridding passengers lined up to board, Maddy started to worry. He'd definitely said to meet him in Glenridding at ten o'clock and her non-transferrable ticket was definitely for this sailing. Her watch was right, there were no messages on her mobile phone, but there was still no signal anyway.

Well, it would just serve him right if she went without him, she thought, loathe to give up her ticket when it was already paid for. As the queue moved Maddy decided she was jolly well going to join it, and she'd make sure she enjoyed the ride too.

As a member of the crew helped her on board she scanned what she could see of Glenridding one last time. Perhaps he'd meet her at Pooley Bridge instead.

Maddy took her seat on the *Raven* so that she was facing towards the wheelhouse. She could just see the back of the skipper's head as he manoeuvred the boat back onto the lake. For a moment she thought he looked just like Jed, but as soon as he spoke into the microphone she knew.

"You devil," she laughed, joining him in the wheelhouse. His face crinkled into a cheeky smile, he was very proud of himself. "Go on then," she continued. "How did you wrangle this?"

"I got a new job," he grinned, briefly checking the dials, twiddling a wheely thing and glancing around.

"But when did you learn to... drive?"

"I've done all the training, and they paid me, too. That's how I could afford the holiday. We won't be rich, but it'll do me, and it beats driving a lorry for a living."

"Well done you," she said, genuinely pleased for him – and for them.

"So, Miss Maddy," said Jed, giving her his full attention for a moment. "Will you marry me?" And he added, "Again?"

The Battle of Killiecrankie

A FINE DAY WELCOMED the Mackenzies to their new home. Blythe Mackenzie, however, was not happy. She'd recently split with her boyfriend and the move had blown all hopes of a reconciliation.

"We'll be closer to your gran's for a start," Jessie Mackenzie had argued. "And Donald will soon settle into his new school – you both will. You'll meet someone else."

"But it won't be Duncan, will it?" wailed Blythe. What did Mum know? It had been ages since she was young or in love. Since Dad died there had been no one.

Mill Cottages stretched out along the roadside just outside Killiecrankie.

"Is this it?" asked Blythe.

"Aye. Aren't they lovely?"

"Which one's ours?"

"The one on the end."

"It's not very big."

"It's got four bedrooms –"

"What do we need four for?"

Jessie sighed. "I can't win. You were always moaning at the other place that there wasn't enough room for all your friends!"

"I won't have that problem here will I? I don't have any friends."

"You will, you'll see," replied Mum, parking the car behind the removals van.

"Has it got a garden?" asked Donald.

"The biggest of the lot," smiled Mum.

"That means me and Mungo can play football." At the sound of his name, the huge mongrel thumped his tail.

"Aye," sighed Mum. "Let's hope the neighbours are friendly."

Soon the removals men were out of their vans, banging and clattering and singing tunelessly to their radio. Donald took Mungo into the back garden.

"What's all this blinking noise?" yelled a man suddenly, dashing from the adjoining cottage.

"Sorry," said Mum.

"You will be. All this crashing and wailing. And what's that barking?"

"That's my son playing with the dog –"

"No one said anything about a dog. You got permission?"

"Well, the deeds said –"

"I hope you know how to control it. How old's your son?"

"Eleven –"

"Young hooligan. I hope you know how to control him too!" He hurried back into his house and slammed the door.

"What was that about neighbours?" asked Blythe.

"Hrmph!" said Mum.

The removals men didn't take long. Jessie paid them and they were on their way, while Blythe went off to explore.

A shop on the corner seemed to sell everything, from toothpaste to magazines.

"Can I help?" asked a lad from behind the counter while Blythe browsed.

"I don't think so. I'm looking for... oh... " She noticed him for the first time. He looked a little older than her, about seventeen, and was very nice. "I was looking for *Red* or *Closer* or something." She needed *something* to keep her occupied in this place.

He pulled a face. "No, we don't have anything like that. But we can get it in. Just moved in today? Mill Cottages are great."

"I wouldn't have thought so myself."

"No?"

"With that miserable old codger living next door?"

He pulled another face to sympathise. "Och, that'll be Mister Sinclair. He's all right really, bark's worse than his bite."

"Well I thought he was very rude." Blythe made to leave the shop but he stopped her.

"What's the name, by the way? For... er... the magazines...?"

"Blythe Mackenzie."

"I'm Jamie Munro," he said, thrusting out his hand.

OVER THE NEXT FEW WEEKS, Mill Cottages became a battleground. If Mum hung out some washing, Mr Sinclair would light a bonfire. If Donald played in the garden, the sprinkler would go on next door. If the family was watching television, he'd switch on his vacuum-cleaner, which interfered with the reception.

Donald had several balls confiscated. When Blythe listened to her CDs he'd bang on the wall, and if she used her hair dryer, he'd come around to complain – because it was interfering with the reception on his television.

"I'm beginning to think this move was a mistake," complained Mum. "Talk about the neighbour from hell. He's even planted some of those leylandii. Four feet a year they grow. We'll lose all of the sunshine in our garden."

"Well, I did warn you," replied Blythe.

"I like it here," said Donald.

"Should be easy enough to sell," mused Mum.

Blythe grinned... Donald groaned.

On Sunday, Blythe took Mungo for a walk along the river. Jamie tagged along too. They walked and chatted for ages, then collapsed on the spongy bank beside a burn. She pulled her sandals off and dipped her feet into the cool, running water.

"This is where it happened," he said.

"What?"

"The Battle of Killiecrankie."

"I thought it was happening down at Mill Cottages."

"He's still playing up then?"

"Aye."

"He'll get fed up."

"Not before us. Why does he do it?"

"He's trying to scare you off."

"He's certainly succeeded." She lay back on the grass and squinted up at the sunny sky.

"What do you mean?"

"Mum's selling up."

"But you've only been here a couple of months."

"I know. It's great, isn't it?"

Jamie frowned. "Don't you like it here?"

"I didn't really want to come."

"So you're leaving?"

Blythe shrugged. "Probably."

"But don't you see? He wants you to leave."

"Why?"

"Because he wants your cottage."

Blythe sat up. "He already has a cottage. Why would he want ours?"

"So he can hire it out as a holiday home."

"Why didn't he buy it then?"

"He tried, but offered far less than the asking price. He thought they wouldn't get a better offer and went off on holiday. Only they did get another offer – yours. He hoped he could be obnoxious enough to frighten you off, your mum would put the place up for sale –"

"– and he'd buy it!" Blythe fumed as she finished the sentence. She jumped to her feet. "He almost got away with it too."

"Almost? But you said your mum –"

"Once I tell her this, she'll change her mind."

LATER THAT AFTERNOON when Blythe and Jessie knew Old Misery would be watching television, Donald was dispatched to the garden and ordered to make as much noise as possible. Blythe switched her CD player on full blast while Jessie 'dried her hair'.

It worked.

Mr Sinclair started banging on the wall as Jessie and Blythe stifled their laughter. They heard his door slam before he came marching up their path. Jessie let him knock for a while before opening the door.

"Sorry Mr Sinclair, I didn't hear the door –"

"I'm not surprised with all this racket going on."

"Did we disturb you? I didn't realise we were making so much noise."

"You should try coming around to my place to listen to it."

"No thanks, I can hear it quite well from here."

"Hrmph! Is that your last word?"

"As a matter of fact it isn't." Mr Sinclair's face dropped. "I know your game. I had my reasons for moving here, and I really thought this would be ideal. Only I didn't bank on you did I? You've made our lives hell since we arrived, and you're not doing it anymore. Any noise you can make, we can make louder. And we'll continue to do so until you get fed up. But you're not getting your greedy little hands on our cottage.

"Now, I'd appreciate it if you got off my step."

To Blythe's surprise, Mr Sinclair didn't say another word. A muscle twitched in his cheek. Suddenly he snorted, spun around and strode back up the garden path, slamming the gate behind him.

"Well," laughed Blythe. "You showed him."

"Hmm," said Jessie thoughtfully. "We might have won the battle, but I don't think we've won the war."

THE REST OF THE SUMMER passed quite peacefully, and then came hallowe'en... but *that* is another story...

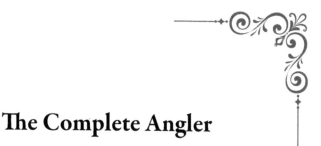

The Complete Angler

THE FISHING SEASON was about to start again but all was not well within the Belshaw family.

"I suppose that means we'll be fending for ourselves again at the weekend," complained daughter Sarah.

"No more lifts on Saturdays to football," moaned Harry, the eldest of the two boys.

"So much for family time," harrumphed Peter, who was really old enough to know better.

Only the youngest, Davey, seemed happy at the prospect. "Leave Mum alone!" he defended. "She does enough for all of us the rest of the week. She's entitled to a day off –"

"But every *week*?" asked Peter, his dad. "It's every week from now until next March."

"That's right!" agreed Sarah. "Honestly, Mum, you can be so selfish!"

"Selfish?" said Jenny. "I'm here every day of the week cooking, cleaning, mending, washing clothes. The beds don't make themselves and, last time I looked, we didn't have a Hoover fairy.

"Not one of you chips in to help. You leave everything to good old muggins."

"But you *are* here all the time," reasoned Harry. "You don't have anything else to do. And fishing's meant to be a man's game anyway."

"Yes," said Sarah. "It's so embarrassing having a mother who goes *fishing*. I have to tell my friends you're meeting Great Aunt Dora in Timbuktu for the day –"

"And they believe *that*?!" asked Jenny, incredulous.

"I think it's cool," said Davey quietly. "And I can't wait until I can go too."

"You'll never get your wheelchair down the bank," joked Harry.

"Harry!" admonished both of his parents at the exact same time.

"I was only kidding," grinned Harry, ruffling his brother's hair, who didn't seem that bothered as he tucked into toast and Marmite.

"The kids might have a point, Jen," said Peter Belshaw finally. "I mean, can we even afford it for a start?"

"Number one," replied Jenny, ticking the item off on her index finger. "It's the only thing I do for myself. The ONLY thing. And number two," she said, ticking her middle finger, "It costs twenty-five pounds. If that. I think you'll find that most other wives are considerably more high maintenance than that."

"But we're saving up to take Davey to America for his operation –"

"And if you want me to go with him then I suggest you let me do this one little thing without complaint. I'll be no good to Davey, or any of you, in a mental institute. Fishing is the only safety valve I have and I'm sick of having this argument with you all every single year.

"Perhaps you'd prefer it if I went to the hairdresser every week instead of washing it myself. Perhaps you'd prefer it if I needed the latest fashions to wear at the school gate. Perhaps you'd prefer it if I liked a bottle of wine every night. I don't drink, I don't smoke, I don't dye my hair, I don't require a Chelsea tractor in which to do the weekly shopping. I fish. And I look after you lot."

Sarah opened her mouth to speak but was silenced by another glare from her mother.

"And I'll have nothing more said on the matter," said Jenny. "One more word and I'm off to live with Great Aunt Dora in Timbuktu."

THE OPENING OF THE new fishing season was greeted with a massive three-day festival and competition sponsored by one of the biggest local tackle manufacturers. First prize was a 16m pole worth more than £3,500.

Jenny sighed. She'd love a brand-new pole of her own for a change, instead of using second-hand or borrowed all of the time, but she knew she could never afford one, and she didn't often win a match. Never mind, she'd enjoy the day sitting on the riverbank, watching the water, battling wits with fish. Not surprisingly, none of the family had ever come to cheer her on, but they'd only be a distraction. Even little Davey.

Jenny sighed again. She didn't know where they'd gone wrong with the other two, but Davey was such a lovely young thing.

The claxon went, marking the start of the contest, and silence descended along the banks of the river. The exhibition ground behind the anglers buzzed softly with visitors, but that was more like white noise for the men and women fishing, and quite calming, actually. Jenny caught a little roach very early on and popped him into her keep net. In a competition like this one on a river where weights weren't generally great, every tiddler counted, and several more followed.

As the sky clouded over and fat drops of rain began to fall, news trickled along the bank that a pike was stealing fish while anglers were reeling them in. Jenny hoped that someone would catch the pike and force it into a sulk before it reached her. They weren't allowed to keep the pike if they caught it, but pike usually lost interest anyway once they've been caught and go and skulk in the shallows in shock for a while.

A journalist bobbed along the bank too, homing in on the more famous anglers for a quick word and a short snap. He didn't recognise Jenny's name on her board but he did hesitate for a while. Jenny concentrated on the water, staring ahead, but as she reeled in another slightly bigger fish, she heard the shutter go on the journalist's camera and smiled to herself. He'd just bagged himself a bit of a novelty. But Jenny knew he'd see other female anglers further down the bank, some of whom had even been on telly.

She was still chuckling quietly to herself when she realised she was actually doing quite well. Probably about ten pound or so, but not bad for a river, and not bad for a woman. The pike must have given her a wide berth, or kept to its own swim.

The river darkened and swelled under the purple cloudy sky and some of the fair-weather anglers started to pack up.

"How have you done?" Jenny asked one of her neighbours.

He shook his head. Not very good," he replied, packing away some of his gear. "I've not caught anywhere near as many as you have," and Jenny bristled slightly with pride. "I'll try again tomorrow."

Jenny would have liked to come back the next day but she'd had her weekly fun. She was content.

As she reeled in her first big catch of the day another one of the early finishers paused pushing his trolley to watch her. When the small carp was safely netted he said: "You've caught more than me in just that one fish."

"Really?" said Jenny. The fish only weighed about four pounds and was just one of her haul. Maybe, just maybe... but she didn't allow herself to go there. Not yet.

THE FINISHING CLAXON sounded and three teams of lads with scales made their way along the riverbank. They weighed Jenny's catch – fourteen pounds. That was a good weight, she realised, especially when it won her the section and then the women's match of the day. But when it beat the men's results too, she was delighted and whooped accordingly. AND she'd won that brand-new pole. "Whoop!" she repeated.

At the award ceremony, all of the runners up in all categories accepted tackle and cheques for their prizes. But when it came to Jenny's turn, she was asked if she wanted the pole or the cash equivalent. What a quandary. However, it didn't take her long to make up her mind. There was no contest.

"I'll take the cash, please," she said, only a little disappointed at not getting the pole. Three thousand five hundred pounds would go a long way to paying for Davey's trip to America, and she told the journalist so too.

BACK HOME PETER BELSHAW could hardly believe it and was overjoyed, for a change.

"See," he said. "I told you all we should let your mum enjoy her little hobby," he grinned. Sarah chucked a cushion at him but Harry tackled him to the floor while Davey giggled his head off.

"And we're going back to the festival with her tomorrow too," announced their dad when he came up for air. "As a family."

THE NEXT MORNING THE Belshaw family returned to the riverbank, sticking to the paths for the most part to accommodate Davey's motorised wheelchair. They played hook-a-duck at one of the stalls, Harry won Sarah a giant teddy bear at the shooting range, and they ate hotdogs and pancakes.

"It's Jenny, isn't it?" said a voice behind them. "Jenny Belshaw?"

"Yes," said Jenny, spinning around to see Tim Avery, owner of the tackle company who were sponsoring the three-day event.

"Congratulations on your win yesterday."

"Thank you."

"I would have liked to have chatted with you but you dashed off in such a hurry."

"Yes, sorry. My family were expecting me home," she explained, sweeping her arm to demonstrate them to him.

"That's okay, we understand," grinned Tim Avery. "And this must be your youngest?" he asked, indicating Davey.

"Er, yes. How did you know?"

"That journalist told me your story, after you'd dashed off."

"Oh," said Jenny, not really sure what else to say.

"And look," said Tim, clearing his throat noisily. "If it's all the same to you, we'd like to give you another prize. We'd like you to accept a fishing pole as well as the cash."

"Oh, er, well... I couldn't really –"

"Nonsense! Of course you can. It's not the same one as yesterday's. We raffled that one off in the end. But if you'd like to accept a different model? It's not as valuable, but still worth almost two thousand pounds..."

He waited expectantly, but Jenny's mouth opened and closed several times with nothing coming out – rather like the fish she caught. And so her husband replied on her behalf.

"She'd like to accept, thank you very much."

"Splendid, splendid," said Tim Avery. And they all shook hands and followed him to the tackle tent.

After the Storm

VIOLET HAD NEVER WANTED to be a grandmother, never wanted to be a mother either. Some mothers were best friends with their daughters. Not Violet. Now the grandchildren were coming, and she never knew what to do with them.

"They only have one grandma," Sarah reminded her once. Tom's parents had been killed in an accident.

"They can't possibly enjoy themselves being stuck here with an old woman."

"They love visiting. You amuse them. You don't fool us. We all know you love us really. You just don't know how to show it. And you're not old. You were only sixteen when you had me."

Violet snorted. She'd never had a grandmother. It hadn't done her any harm. She didn't even have a mother. Her mother had deserted her when she was hours old.

VIOLET HEARD THE CAR doors slam. Her daughter hadn't wasted any time getting here. Sarah let them all in with her own key, and the children rushed towards Violet with out-stretched arms. But she felt so awkward with them.

"Sorry to dump them on you, Mum."

"You're looking very nice." She was tall, blonde and slim – like her father. She didn't look thirty-five. "Interview?"

"Can we have a drink, please Gran?" asked Bethany.

47

"Is there any squash?" asked Matthew.

Violet made her own lemon cordial. The children loved it, and she always kept some in, in case they dropped by. "You know where it is," she said, and they rushed off.

"Just business," replied Sarah finally. She tucked a silvery strand of hair behind her ear.

"When will you be back?"

"A couple of hours. Just plonk them in front of Children's Television."

As Sarah kissed the children Violet pursed her lips. Her favourite soap was on this afternoon. She should have got a DVD player like Matthew had urged, or at least another television.

Before Sarah had closed the door behind her, the children were sitting in front of the telly. "Haven't you got Sky yet?" asked Matthew. "They have some brill programmes."

Matthew was eleven. His voice was at that cracked stage, and ugly spots were threatening his complexion.

"Don't be silly, Matt," laughed Bethany, who was seven. "Granny only got Freeview because they made her."

The children soon became engrossed in a cartoon. Violet watched them. They both wore good clothes, as usual. She wondered how much Sarah had paid for those. Violet sniffed. Sarah had had to make do with second-hand stuff, as had her mother previously.

Violet picked up some knitting but put it down again. It was too humid. Maybe she'd get herself some of that cordial.

"Do you two want another drink?" she asked, moving out to the kitchen.

"Yes please," said both voices simultaneously.

She opened the fridge door and heard a distant rumble. At first she thought she was mistaken, but no, that was definitely another. The children were too busy with their programme to notice the thunder growling in the background. But Violet hadn't missed it. She crept to the window to see the mauve clouds piling up on the horizon. Violet couldn't help feeling anxious. She hated thunderstorms...

Bethany and Matthew looked on in surprise as Violet hurried about the place. "What're you doing?" asked Matthew quietly.

"Switching off the electrical appliances," she replied, pulling the plug on the telly.

"Why?" asked Bethany.

"Because of the storm." The children exchanged a puzzled look. "You'll have to play cards instead."

Accustomed to their grandmother's occasional eccentricities, Bethany and Matthew duly began a game of Snap!, which was one game Bethany knew how to play. But when they spotted Violet making sure the windows were all open... "What're you doing that for, Granny?" asked the girl.

"To let the lightning through the house."

"Oh," she said, seeming to stick to her grandmother's old rule that children should be seen and not heard.

"Snap!" cried Matthew suddenly while Bethany wasn't concentrating.

"That's not fair!"

"Too bad. I win," he grinned.

As the children played, Violet gazed out of the lounge window at the purple sky. That's what she'd been named after all those years ago by the people at the orphanage. Well, they didn't exactly call her 'purple', but they did choose the name 'Violet'. And, short of any further inspiration, her surname became 'Smith'.

A brilliant flash of light split the sky. Violet felt all the muscles in her body tense as she waited for the subsequent clap of thunder. There had been a dreadful storm that night too, when Violet's mother had forsaken her. She felt herself trembling and close to tears every time she thought of that word, forsaken. It sounded cold and empty. A fine word for someone abandoned to an orphanage and a foster home, and ending up in a juvenile centre. Thunderstorms always brought the memories tumbling back.

Forsaken, that's what she'd been. At least until Danny came along, another orphan in a storm. He was handsome. Tall, slim, blond. He made her feel special. Told her she was beautiful, that he loved her. And she believed him. For once in her life someone cared, and she trusted him.

But where was Danny when she found out she was pregnant? He'd already disappeared. And there was that word again, forsaken. Violet Smith was meant to be alone. The foster family sent her to a special hostel for single mothers.

Then history almost repeated itself. Her baby was only a few hours old when Violet dressed herself and walked out of the hospital. Outside, there was a storm raging. The lightning flashed, thunder roared and the rain fell so hard it hurt.

Violet was frozen with fear. She was getting soaked, but she couldn't go forward and she couldn't go back. She simply stood there sobbing loudly. Eventually, one of the sisters found her there. They made it back to her baby and she climbed back into bed. They called it post-natal depression these days, she'd seen a programme on the telly just the other day... and then she wondered if that's what had been wrong with her own mother.

VIOLET FLINCHED. THE storm was overhead now. She felt a tiny hand slip into her own and Bethany's big brown eyes looked up at hers, full of concern. "Don't worry, Granny. It's only God shouting at the angels for switching the lights on and off."

"Where on earth did you get that from?"

"From Daddy, of course. Look, the angels are crying now."

Violet didn't need to see the rain that was now falling. She could smell it on the grass through the open windows.

"Now," continued Bethany, tugging at Violet's hand. "You must come away from the window. If God sees you watching, he might shout at you too."

What a delightful interpretation, thought Violet, as she allowed the girl to drag her away. All her life she'd been afraid of thunderstorms, and here was a child telling her not to worry.

"You do talk rubbish at times," said Matthew. "Everybody knows it's a single discharge of electricity that causes thunder and lightning –"

"I think I prefer Bethany's definition, thank you," said Violet. "Now, about this game of Snap!..."

While they played the storm flashed and grumbled, rain hammered against the roof. Matthew closed the windows as Bethany fetched more cordial. By the time Sarah returned, Violet was sad to see them go.

"You will bring them again?"

Sarah gave her mother a quizzical look. "Of course. Are you okay?"

"Never felt better," replied Violet, smiling after the children as they climbed into the car. "They've been looking after me. How did your day go?"

"It was fine."

"You going to tell me about it?"

"I'm not sure you'd like it. I've been trying to locate my dad –"

"What?"

"He *is* my dad –"

"It's a pity he didn't remember that when he walked out on me."

"We don't know that he did. You always assumed that. But did he even know about me?"

Violet opened her mouth to argue, and then closed it again, thoughtfully. Her daughter just might have a point. Did she even get a chance to tell Danny about the baby?

"I'll need your help, Mum," said Sarah, softly.

It was too much for one day. Violet didn't know what to believe. Her whole world had changed: first the children, then the storm, and now this...

AFTER THE STORM THERE was a rainbow. Violet watched from her lounge window. Of course she would help Sarah find her dad – if she could. But it would take time to get used to the idea.

She smiled. She still hated storms, that would never change. But they did always seem to be around whenever there was a major change in her life. At least she knew now that she did have people to love her. They'd been there all along.

Autumn

EMMA, this flash story won first prize in a competition
TRICK OR TREAT, first published in *Twee Tales Too*
BURN, this story won second prize in a competition

Emma

EMMA PICKED HER WAY along the cliff's edge.

Coastguards practised beyond on the stormy sea. Seagulls soared overhead. Emma envied them their freedom, finally acknowledging how trapped she felt.

It was time. Her dad would manage.

She stepped off the cliff, plunged into the sea... and hoped the coastguard wouldn't notice.

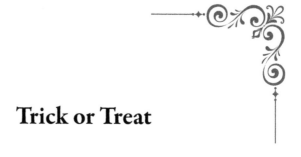

Trick or Treat

THOMAS STOOD AT HIS new bedroom window staring across the village green towards the small parish church and its graveyard beyond. He couldn't actually see it from where he was standing, apart from a corner of the church's Norman tower (he knew it was Norman because they'd told them in class), but he knew it was there and, more importantly, *they* knew that *he* was there. They'd woken him up in the night.

"What happened this time?" asked his mum as she sorted out some clothes for him to wear.

"Dead mummies," he said, shuddering at the memory. "All the old graves opened and out came a load of dead mummies looking for children who weren't asleep."

"You're doing Ancient Egypt at school now, then?" asked his mum.

He turned and looked at her in surprise, eyes wide. *His* mum seemed to know *every*thing. "How did *you* know *that*?" he said. "We only started yesterday."

"Because we don't have mummies in England, let alone any dead ones. But they do in Ancient Egypt."

"Oh," he said, turning back to the window. "So how did they get into *our* graveyard? Did they dig a tunnel all the way from Egypt?"

"No they didn't. It was just another bad dream. I'll have to see about finding you a dreamcatcher. That imagination of yours is amazing."

Thomas dressed himself while his mum straightened the bed clothes. "Ellie's going Trick or Treating on Thursday and she says I'm to go with her. "Can I please, Mummy?"

"You must be joking," she laughed. "You'll have nightmares about monsters for weeks if you do that."

"Don't be silly, Mummy. It'll only be us dressed up as monsters. There won't be any *real* monsters. And Ellie says that the villagers will be so scared of us that they'll give us sweeties and chocolates just to go away, and some will even give us 20p. How can I have nightmares about children dressed up in silly costumes and sweeties and chocolates and 20ps?"

"Well, when you put it like that..."

He knew his mum was thinking about it. He'd never been Trick or Treating before and it sounded like fun. Everything here was still new to him and everything here was fun.

"Some of the older children will take us around if you're too scared to, but it's only the village. It's not like where we used to live.

"Can I please, Mum? Can I?"

"THERE'S NO SUCH THING as dead mummies," said Ellie at school later that day. "Or ghosties and ghoulies or proper monsters. They're *always* just people dressed up in silly costumes trying to scare other people. I bet if you punched one of your mummies in your dream on the nose, it would just disappear in a cloud of dust. *Poof!*"

"But why do people want to scare other people if it isn't Trick or Treat night?" asked Thomas, before taking a bite from his apple and then munching noisily.

"For fun. Because they're nasty bullies and like to frighten people. Because they're greedy and want to steal or keep something valuable to themselves. To make little children do as they're told. Lots of reasons. Haven't you ever seen *Scooby Doo*?"

Thomas had his mouth full so just shook his head sadly.

"You can watch it at mine. I have loads on DVD. And if you still don't believe me, I'll prove it to you when we go Trick or Treating. There will be lots of us."

Thomas could hardly wait. It all sounded very exciting.

AFTER WATCHING SEVERAL *Scooby Doos* at Ellie's, the two of them spent a couple of days pretending they were solving mysteries, just like those 'pesky kids'. Thomas was Shaggy, because he thought he was funny, and Ellie played Velma, because they had the same hair colour. They also had some ideas for their Halloween costumes. Ellie was going to be a mummy, but not a dead one, to prove her point to Thomas. She raided her mum's industrial-sized first aid box for bandages of all sizes. Thomas was going to be a skeleton. His mum was making the costume for him.

On Halloween night they were teamed up with a couple of older sisters, Kitty (a witch) and Claire (a lady vampire), whose parents were on the village committee. Armed with water pistols and buckets for goodies, off they went, along with most of the other village children in their little clusters. It was a like a big outdoor party.

"Trick or Treat!" they shouted, or they roared or growled whenever someone opened a door. Thomas was delighted when *all* of the villagers they saw were genuinely frightened to see them standing on their doorsteps and only too eager to fill their buckets with chewy sweets and lollipops to make them go away. A few householders ignored them, but the older girls had warned them that some might. So they squirted their front windows with their water pistols. Other houses were in total darkness. They passed a lot of their friends in the lanes and had fun guessing who they were and what they were dressed up as. And all around, the darkened village was illuminated by lanterns of various shapes and sizes, glowing like fairy lights at Christmas.

"See," said Ellie. "Just people dressed up in silly costumes, just like us. There's no such thing as ghosties and ghoulies and monsters and mummies."

"But we haven't been anywhere near the graveyard yet," protested Thomas. He wanted to see it in the dark to see if it was as scary as in his dreams. "That's where the *real* dead mummies keep coming from."

"We can go back that way if you want," said Kitty the witch.

"Some of us are meeting there later," said Claire the lady vampire. "When we've finished at your party, at the welfare hall, the rest of us have a party in the church yard."

"We can go that way if you want," agreed Ellie, the live mummy.

Thomas felt butterflies in his tummy. It was dark and damp and a little bit foggy by now, muffling their footsteps and making the other children sound further away. He imagined all sorts of beasties lurking in the graveyard at night, but he was supposed to be *his* mummy's brave little soldier...

"Look," said Kitty. "If anything jumps out at you, just yell as loud as you can. It'll soon run away."

"Or punch it on the nose," reminded Ellie.

And so the four of them turned towards the church yard to take a shortcut to the miners' welfare hall. Thomas noticed that Ellie was clinging to him as tightly as he was clinging to her, but they were both awestruck when they did reach the graveyard.

The old church building was illuminated from below by soft, orange lighting, picking out all of the shadows and carvings. There were more pumpkin lanterns casting mini pools of light along the footpath that wound around the old building and into the yard itself, with some hanging from the old lychgate roof, and up the steps leading to the church main door. But aside from that some of the graves and tombs had tiny solar-powered lights of their own twinkling in the darkness, and a wind chime hanging from a tree tinkled softly.

It didn't look like a graveyard where monsters and mummies lived. It looked like a magical fairyland. And nothing jumped out at them from behind any headstones.

THE OLDER KIDS HELPED to supervise the youngsters at their village Halloween party back at the welfare hall. There was a disco with coloured and silver balls swinging from the ceiling, dancing, a soft drinks table, a running buffet, and lots of seasonal games contests, like apple bobbing (in water and in flour), blind man's bluff, charades and conkers. And they had toffee apples and hotdogs to eat.

THOMAS SLEPT SURPRISINGLY well that night without a single nightmare. The next time he did dream about dead mummies coming to take him underground, all the way back to Egypt, he tried yelling at them in his dream, as loudly as he could, but nothing came out. He panicked momentarily and then punched one of the mummies right on the nose, and it disappeared in a cloud of dust. *Poof!*

Oh, he liked that one. But he was never troubled by nightmares ever again, which disappointed him because he wanted to punch them all on the nose...

Burn

WHEN MARCIE CRAIG ARRIVED home in the early hours of the morning, the last thing she expected to find was a dead body. Well, not really a body. More a smouldering mass with two skinny legs sticking out.

Obligatory vomiting over, Marcie called the police.

The body turned out to be Ivy Dennis, an old friend of Marcie's – and a somewhat older resident of the caravan site they both shared. After the inquest, Marcie couldn't believe the verdict.

"Spontaneous human combustion?" she scoffed over a pint at her local. "No such thing."

"It's what the coroner thinks," explained her mate Reefer, a policeman. "And let's face it," he continued, "what else could it be?"

"Could've been murder. Could've wanted to hide the evidence."

"Who'd want to murder an old biddy like that?" He finished his own pint and signalled for another round.

"Could've been a robbery gone wrong –"

"Robbery!" Now it was Reefer's turn to laugh. "What did she have to rob? No money, a rented caravan, no relatives –"

"Actually," said Marcie getting excited, "she had a niece – and she must've had money somewhere... I witnessed her will."

Reefer paid for the drinks. "Who was the main beneficiary?"

"The Cats Protection League."

He shrugged. "So where's the motive? I can't see them murdering an old woman just to get their hands on her cash. Can you?"

Marcie paused and took advantage of her new pint. "I dunno... I haven't thought that far ahead."

Reefer laughed again, downed his pint and stood up to leave. "Marcie, leave the sleuthing to the professionals and get on with being a DJ." That was the trouble with Marcie Craig. She couldn't keep her nose out of anything. And besides, Ivy was a friend.

Marcie had lived on the site for more than fifteen years, although Ivy had been there a lot longer. She was a pensioner and had lived in her caravan for most of her life. Cutler had inherited Ivy as a sitting tenant when he bought the place, so was she paying a peppercorn rent? Marcie wondered. How about that for a motive? She decided to have tea with the delightful chap to find out what he'd been doing all those Saturdays ago.

Cutler mused, rubbing his bristly chin with a hairy finger. "Wasn't that the night you found Ivy Dennis in your garage?" Marcie nodded encouragement and stirred three sugars into the tea that was too strong. "What's it to you anyway?"

"Nothing really," she shrugged. "It just seems strange, I wondered if anyone noticed anything unusual. Like what was she doing there anyway?"

"I see what you mean." He scratched noisily at his chin again and dunked (and dropped) a chocolate biscuit in his tea. "It's no good," he announced finally, fishing out the soggy biscuit with a teaspoon. "I'll have to check the dates." To save time, Marcie furnished him with them and, to her dismay, his face lit up.

"We had a little competition at the golf club. I won and had all my drinks bought for me." He chuckled at the memory. "I was well-oiled. They had to put me up for the night."

She gave up on the tea, thanked him warmly for his hospitality and left. On her way home, Marcie noticed a girl leaving Ivy's ancient caravan.

"Hallo," she called out. "It's Angela, isn't it? Ivy's niece?"

The girl nodded and reluctantly made her way towards Marcie.

"Marcie Craig –"

"Aunty used to talk about you."

The two women stood awkwardly in the middle of the park, the visitor seeming eager to get away.

Marcie said, "You been tidying up?"

"No. The place is locked. I don't think I could face it anyway."

"I'm really very sorry about your aunt."

"Thank you. I just wish I'd seen her, you know, before it happened."

"It's been a while then?"

Angela sighed. "About three months."

"Well, I won't keep you. I can see you're dying to get away –" Marcie could have kicked herself at her choice of words. Nevertheless, they made leaving noises and went in different directions.

Marcie had a key. Not that Ivy locked the place that often. However, she had entrusted her friend with a key rather than her only surviving relative, and that started alarm bells ringing.

Ivy's van smelled musty and airless but there was still a faint reminder of the old lady's favourite perfume. Ornaments were neatly in place covered with a fine layer of dust. Marcie started bagging clothes and rubbish. She came across a pile of diaries dating back to the 1950s. Marcie kept those for herself – they might make interesting reading and had been kept right up until Ivy's death.

Out of some morbid interest, she dipped into the past few weeks leading up to the 'accident' and discovered a startling fact. Ivy was spying on the neighbours and keeping detailed records of all their comings and goings – even Marcie was there. She found it quite amusing reading about herself from an outsider's point of view, but the second startling fact was that Mr Mills, the friendly, loveable site manager, was having a sordid affair behind his crippled wife's back with the sixteen-year-old at number twenty. Time for another invite to tea, she thought.

"It's good to see you, Marcie," said Mr Mills. Everyone called him that and she had no idea what his first name was. He shifted around the kitchen making much nicer coffee than Cutler's tea had been, and took one through to his invalid wife who called hello to Marcie through the door. "We were away," he replied finally, after Marcie had explained her visit. "Jenny gets Respite care and I often go with her."

Marcie lowered her voice so that Jenny wouldn't hear what she had to say. "Did you know Ivy was spying on us all?"

Mr Mills threw back his head and laughed. "Yes. The daft old bat accused me of seeing young Gillian across the way," he indicated with his finger. "Jenny thought it was hilarious – particularly as the girl's parents were there every time I went. I've been teaching her French, you know. A bit of extra help before her exams."

Marcie didn't know whether to feel frustrated or relieved, but she settled on the latter because it was the thing to do. When she returned to her own van, she continued reading Ivy's diaries until the day of her death.

In between those pages was a letter from Angela demanding that Ivy change her will back, otherwise she would contest the thing, citing senility or something. Ivy had apparently found this quite amusing, but had agreed to see her niece nonetheless... on the evening that she died...

MARCIE WAS VERY IMPRESSED with Reefer's ability to get the case re-examined. "You've done a grand job," she congratulated.

"You didn't do so badly yourself," he grinned, over the top of one of their endless pints.

"Of course, I don't believe Angela really meant her aunt any harm," she said. "Ivy was frail and possibly did fall. But to do something like that? Ugh."

"Frightened," Reefer stated. "Imagine the strength she would have needed to drag the body down to the garage? She probably didn't expect it to burn all night."

"Pah!" exclaimed Marcie. "Spontaneous human combustion? No such thing."

Winter

DON'T BREAK A LEG, first published in *Twee Tales Too*
BREAKING THE ICE, first published in *Twee Tales Too*
DANCING ON ICE, first published in *Twee Tales Too*

Don't Break a Leg

WHEN DAN SAW THE DUMP of snow they'd had overnight, he made a silent prayer of thanks. He'd taken the kids away for a winter holiday to the country and was slowly running out of things to do. He'd seen a sledge in the cottage's garage and hadn't given it a second thought. Until now.

"C'mon kids," he yelled up the stairs. "Breakfast is ready and then we're off out."

But the girls didn't need calling twice. They'd seen the snow and ran squealing down the stairs, eager to get into the tiny garden and make a snowman. Or even a snow lady, they chattered.

"Don't wolf your food," he reminded them, but was delighted to see the looks of happiness on their little faces. They hadn't had a great time since their mum had died, but he was doing his best. Heck, it hadn't been a sleigh-ride for him either.

"We can make a snowman and a snow lady and a snow dog –" said Matty around a mouthful of toast.

"And then we can make a giant snowball and make it bigger and bigger by rolling it everywhere," agreed her older sister Suze. She mopped up her runny egg with a piece of toast, jumped up from the table and placed her plate carefully into the sink.

"And then we can have a snowball fight," said Matty, copying Suze. She always copied anything her big sister did.

"Hey, and how about we go sledging?" suggested their dad, cleaning up after the pair of them.

"Sledging?" said Suze, already-big eyes opening even wider.

"Yay!" said Matty, copying her sister's facial expression.

He sent them back upstairs to dress themselves in their warmest clothes while he loaded the dishwasher with crocks from the sink and made them a picnic of hot baked beans in a flask, bread and butter, and chocolate cake slices. Dan had no idea where they would go or how long they'd be, so he also made sure his phone was charged and he had plenty of money in his pockets.

By the time the girls came back down the stairs he had a large-scale Ordnance Survey map of the local area spread out across the newly scrubbed kitchen table.

"Where are we going?" asked Suze, coming to look at the map. After teaching her to read, the next thing Dan did was show his eldest daughter how to read a simple roadmap. The Ordnance Survey map was far too complicated for her but she'd already started to identify some of the symbols and she knew that red bendy lines usually meant big hills.

"That bit looks green," she said, pointing to an actually quite green part of the map.

"That looks green," mimicked her little sister, pointing at what was actually a disused mine workings.

He laughed at the two of them but actually they hadn't done too badly at all. There was a wood, a country park, a reservoir and a visitor centre situated almost on top of a disused mine workings, and if there was still an old slagheap there, that would be ideal sledging terrain. And all within walking distance too, in case he couldn't get the car out...

... which, of course, he couldn't.

The garage wasn't much more than a glorified shed and was currently beneath the biggest snowdrift Dan had ever seen. He was able to get in – just about – to get to the sledge. But the car wasn't having any of it. And besides, he didn't want to waste valuable snow time digging out a car that may not get up the track anyway.

He buttoned up the girls' coats, and checked their gloves and scarves were on tight and secure. Then he hitched the small rucksack onto his back and dragged the sledge behind him with his free hand. His other hand clasped one of Matty's, and Matty's free hand grabbed at one of Suze's. And so, in their wellies, they tramped a path through the virgin snow onto what Dan hoped was the grass verge beneath. That was the trouble when it snowed, you had to be careful you didn't break your leg stepping onto what you thought was solid ground, but what in fact could turn out to be a ditch or a hole.

Once he was sure there was no danger of any traffic on the country roads, he allowed the girls to run on ahead, taking great delight in trashing the brand-new snow. A stray snowball almost reached them from someone else's snowball fight, so they spent a few minutes laughing and squealing and joining in.

"Good morning!" said almost every single person they saw, and Dan mused more than once that this wouldn't be the case in town. He asked one local the best way to the nearest hills and the chap confirmed he was on the right path.

"There's a snicket in between the houses opposite where this road comes out at the top. That'll take you to the playground and you'll see the woods on the other side of the park." All the while the man gave his directions, he waved his arms, and Matty stood behind him copying him. "You'll lose your mobile phone signal in the woods, but keep to the right-hand side, close to the edge, until you can see a stile. That'll take you out of the woods, up along the path and onto the top of the muckheap. There'll be loads of others up there today," he added, looking at the sky. "And there's more snow to come."

Dan thanked the man and they continued on their way. But it was unlikely they'd get lost as, just as the man had said, lots of others had the same idea. There were plenty of dads and lads and kids with sleds, even if they weren't all going in the same direction.

"Ooh," squealed Matty when she saw the playground. "Can we go on the jumble jim?"

"Can we go on the seesaw?" chimed in her sister.

"Can we go on the slide?" asked Matty.

"Yes," laughed their dad, taking advantage of a break in the trek. There were other children here already and the snow had mostly been cleared or trod away by them. "Be careful, though," he called after them. "You don't want to be breaking a leg."

"Breaking a leg!" mimicked Matty.

Matty did a few gambols around one of the *jungle gym* bars and Dan was relieved she'd chosen to wear her corduroy jeans instead of the short skirt and woolly tights she usually favoured. It wasn't long before she realised her big sister was doing something different to her, and she followed her around the playground, up the steps and down the slide. And when they were bored of that, they headed across the park, along a path in the snow that had already started to form, despite the snow reaching almost to the tops of their wellies.

Their dad had carried on walking slowly towards the woods while keeping a very firm eye on them both and they caught him up. Through a kissing gate they went, into the trees their friendly neighbour had promised would be there.

Once inside the woods, however, Dan started to lose his bearings. The snow had drifted quite deeply but already a few children had trampled several paths. Not being at all familiar with the place he had no idea where the actual path was and which one was the right one.

"Keep to the right," the man had said. But how far right? Did the path run along the outside edge of the woods or the inside edge or deeper into the wood? Was there a dyke? Were there brambles or rabbit holes?

In order to keep the children safe – and himself – he had two choices: go back, or follow one of the already trampled paths.

Common sense told him to go back. The dad wanted to give his children a good time. But which path should Good Time Charlie take? And would he lose face if he went back?

Matty suddenly scampered off after a squirrel, but when she noticed that no one was following her, she went back and copied her sister copying their dad, legs akimbo, hands on hips.

"Which way do we go?" asked Suze.

"Good question," said Dan.

"The middle!" said Matty.

What the hell, thought Dan. How lost could they get in such a small wood.

"Come on, then," he exclaimed, leading the way so he could test for holes and tree roots first. If they *did* get lost it would be easy to re-trace their steps. "Keep close behind," he called, dragging the sledge behind him over the bumps. "Don't –"

"Break a leg!" chimed the girls together.

"It's turning into an enchanted forest," squealed Suze.

"Chanted forest," echoed her sister.

"Perhaps we'll see Little Red Riding Hood –"

"Ding Hood!"

As the girls chattered and fantasised, Dan tried to concentrate on the path. The middle definitely followed a regular trail, but it was so hard to keep his bearings. The wood got denser and thicker, blocking out the weak winter sunshine. But the footprints he followed were numerous and of different shapes and sizes. Either a few people had already come this way this morning or the same few had been running around in circles.

The light grew brighter again but it turned out to be just a clearing. Perhaps this was the centre and they only had the same distance again to trek through.

"Ooh!" exclaimed Suze. "A witch's clearing –"

"Chis clearing," echoed Matty, running up to the stump of what was once a big old tree. Sawn.

"Perhaps this is their sacrificial altar," wondered Suze, spinning around while looking up at the sky.

At least the sun was still shining, thought Dan, wondering which path to take next.

Matty stooped down to examine the snow. "Is that a paw print?" she asked.

"It's a hoof," sad her dad. "There must be deer in here."

"Oh dear," said Suze, and both girls fell into helpless giggles. It was great to hear them laugh. The walk had been worth it just for that.

"C'mon," he said, taking the most trampled path right opposite the one they'd emerged from.

And the girls followed him, chuntering on between them about going on a bear hunt.

"Oh-ka-ay," said Suze.

"Okay!" replied her sister.

"Let's go!"

"Let's go!" echoed Matty.

Before long they re-emerged from the wood... back into the witch's clearing.

"Oh dear," said Matty, mimicking her sister from earlier. And they both dissolved into fits of giggles again.

We should have gone back, thought Dan. Or stuck to the edge of the wood. Now he didn't know which was the path they'd come in on earlier, nor which was the one he'd taken. There was one less trampled path left, though, so he decided to take that one.

And that took them back to where they'd started.

"Shall we try sledging another day?" he asked at last.

"There might not be any snow another day," mused Suze.

"Don't you know the way?" asked his younger daughter.

"Not really," he admitted, while silently admonishing himself for being so irresponsible. Anything could have happened – they could have fallen down a hole or tripped over some brambles and done some real damage. Or they could have been stranded, lost in the smallest wood on the planet... and now he was being melodramatic.

"Let's go back to that playground and start again," he said at last.

And they left the wood through the kissing gate and headed back across the field. It was busier now, with more families enjoying the sunshine.

"We're going up the muckstack now," said one of the older boys. "You can come with us if you like."

They were a mixed group, age and gender, but they seemed nice children, and one of them had a small dog with her, a mongrel. "If we show you the way," she said, "maybe we can have a go on your sledge?"

"What do you two think?" he asked Suze and Matty, who both agreed with a cheer.

And so Dan and the girls went with the village children around the outside edge of the wood and in only minutes they were on the other side of the trees and already part-way up a snow-covered slagheap.

"Wow," said Suze.

"Wow," mimicked Matty.

And they chased the other children and the dog up the hill leaving poor old Dan to drag the wooden sledge behind him.

They all had lots of fun sliding down the hillside, on plastic, brightly coloured sledges; on faithful, sturdy wooden hand-made sledges; even on their backsides – although someone was obviously wearing brand new jeans as they'd managed to leave a dark blue trail in the snow everywhere they went. Even the adults who were with them joined in.

Dan was content. The girls had new friends to play with for the rest of their holiday and Dan had been invited out for a drink.

On the way back to the cottage, after they'd said their goodbyes, Dan slipped on a patch of frozen snow, landed with a thump, and twisted his ankle after all. But at least it wasn't broken and he'd mend, just like his heart had already started to mend.

The dark days were almost over. It was time to live again.

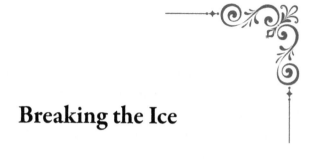

Breaking the Ice

STEVIE HAD WORKED FREELANCE from home for such a long time even the neighbours had got used to it. Now she looked at all the grubby snow piled around her poor little car. It was all very well them having these little street-clearing parties, but how was she supposed to even open the car door? The road was almost clear of snow so all the others had been able to get their cars out and go to work or school or wherever. But it was still several feet high in places and *her* car was lost beneath it all.

"It's a good job you don't have to be anywhere important," laughed Merv at number twenty-eight. He had his dogs with him – three rottweilers and a labrador – so they must have been off out for a walk.

"Actually, I start my new job this morning," she replied, dejected.

"Oh dear," said Merv. "Look, I'll get a couple of shovels. We'll have you out of there in no time."

Stevie felt quite guilty for always avoiding him now. He could be quite creepy at times, though, a bit over-familiar at others. But perhaps it was shyness that made him come across as quite odd.

They'd already made good work of the piles of snow when Gary from the big house joined them. The neighbours had piled snow across the end of his drive too, so he couldn't get out either. He obviously knew how she felt.

After about ten minutes the three of them had cleared a car-wide space that both she and Gary could get through. Merv, meanwhile, went back to collect his dogs again so he could take them for that walk.

"Thanks," she called out to him as she pushed her car key into the door. But as she tried to turn the key, she realised the lock was frozen – and her de-icer was inside the car.

Gary from the big house crept past her and called through his open window. "You could do with some de-icer on that," he suggested. Then he drove off.

"Yeah, thanks," muttered Stevie, stomping the snow off her boots as she went back into the house to fetch the kettle. She used the still-warm water on her car windows and left the engine running as she popped the kettle back into the kitchen. By the time she got back to her car the ice had cleared but the windows were steamed up.

"Damn! Damn! Damn!" she complained, cranking the demister fan into life. She'd started the day in such a good mood too, and in such good time, excited about starting her new job. And now the shine was coming off it the more tetchy she became.

The little nondescript Saxo took its sweet time warming up after both being stood for several days *and* beneath a pile of cold, wet snow. But it kangarooed up the hill for Stevie to find the main roads clear. Totally and utterly clear, and with a normal flow of traffic. A low-slung sun temporarily blinded her and she had to stop the car at the next junction longer than strictly necessary for fear of hitting something she may not be able to see or – worse – someone. A horn blared from behind her at the same time she heard their brakes screech.

Oh dear, she thought. Her first day back in the rat race wasn't going well at all.

As she joined the traffic on the top road, Merv and his dogs emerged from the top end of the snicket, and he gave her a cheery wave. She twiddled the knob on her radio to tune into one of the new local DAB channels and promptly got stuck behind a bus that had stopped between stops so that Old Mrs Blake could climb aboard. While it was very nice for the local bus drivers to be so helpful to the village's elderly residents, it wasn't helping Stevie get to work on time. And what was

Old Mrs Blake doing getting on a bus so early anyway? Surely her bus pass didn't start until 9:30am...

Stevie checked the clock on her dashboard to make sure she wasn't actually *that* late. Phew! Only 8:35am. It was a good job she'd given herself plenty of time. But what *was* the old woman doing catching a bus at this time of the day? Perhaps she always did, Stevie scolded herself. After all, Stevie was the one not normally out and about at this time of the day. Maybe Old Mrs Blake was.

She drummed her fingers on the steering wheel, admonishing herself for getting so close to the stupid bus in the first place. Tyre and tarmac, she muttered to herself. Tyre and tarmac. Always leave enough room in case the person in front decides to have a picnic. If she didn't get around the bus soon she really *was* going to be late. Proper late.

This particular bus driver was clearly stopping to have a picnic while he waited for Old Mrs Blake to sit herself down. Or he was waiting for more latecomers – or early birds, depending on which bus they wanted. So Stevie checked her rear-view mirror, reversed up, and swerved around the parked bus, narrowly missing another bus coming in the opposite direction, while Old Mrs Blake's bus driver honked his horn at her.

Twenty-to-nine. If there were no other obstructions she might just make it. Stevie didn't want to make the call on her mobile phone just yet, in case anyone else was running late. She didn't see the point in drawing attention to her own shoddy timekeeping if no one else was in either. And anyway, in her rush she'd forgotten to activate her hands-free. No fancy integrated devices in this old car.

The dual-carriageway was even clearer than the other main roads. If it was like this all the way she'd have a job convincing anyone she'd been snowed in. There was quite a lot of sludgy, slushy, dirty water lying in puddles at the road's edge, though, some reaching almost to the middle of the carriageway.

Up ahead of her Stevie could see a clumsily parked sports car with the bonnet up half-abandoned in a snow-covered layby and half jutting out into the main road. A woman with a bright yellow woollen hat on to match her car, and a long, red coat, stood at the roadside frantically waving for someone to stop and help push her precious car to safety. Normally Stevie would have been first in the queue, but she simply didn't have the time today. Because she felt guilty, she tried to avert her glance from the woman's as she drove past, even though she could feel the woman's eyes glaring right at her. As she checked her rear-view mirror, she was mortified to see that she'd not only ignored the poor thing but also driven through a mucky puddle and splashed her from head to foot.

"Damn!" she said again, feeling more guilty than ever.

Stevie pulled into the car park at *Paranormal Investigations Monthly Magazine* and was relieved to see that in between several heaps of shovelled snow there was just one car parking space left. It was two minutes to nine o'clock. She'd only just made it.

ABOUT THIRTY MINUTES after Mr Brookes, her new boss, had shown her to her workstation, Stevie was making a cup of tea when she heard a commotion around the clocking-in clock. Through the window Stevie could see the roof of a bright yellow convertible abandoned in the car park, and at the clock stood a woman in a bright yellow woollen hat – to match her car – and a long, mud-soaked, once-red coat. She was complaining very loudly, and very indignantly.

"... and then the ignorant cow bounced through a puddle and splashed me from head to toe."

Stevie hunkered down behind her desk where she could watch what looked like the honey monster from the Sugar Puffs adverts remove her wet things. She didn't remove the bright yellow woollen hat, though. That turned out to be her hair.

"Ah, you're here," said Mr Brookes, coming out to greet the latecomer. "Come and meet Stephanie." He fetched the honey monster as he spoke. "Stephanie, this is Tina. She's going to show you the ropes and you'll report to her. She's been a bit, ah, delayed by this morning's..."

"You?!" screeched the honey monster as Stevie straightened up behind her desk and plastered a smile across her face. "YOU?" shrieked the monster.

Oh dear, thought Stevie. Not the best way to break the ice in her new job. Boy, was this going to be a fun ride...

Dancing on Ice

DAN'S HEART SANK TO the pit of his stomach. These were yet more of the times he missed his late wife, not having her there for the girls. He'd promised his oldest daughter a treat of her choice for getting another sticker at school, and Suze had chosen ice skating.

"Loads of my friends are going," she'd said. "And it looks so easy on television."

Easy?! Pah! Pull the other one. Dan remembered his own attempts at ice skating only too well. While most of his friends were trialling for the ice hockey or speed skating teams, poor Dan was spending most of his time cold, wet, bruised and on his backside. Not to mention the ego-bashing and leg-pulling he'd also experienced.

Ice skating never was and never would be for him. But he *had* promised...

"Can I go too?" asked his younger daughter Matty.

Dan wasn't sure if there was a minimum age or not for ice skating at the local rink. He had a dim and distant recollection that there was a minimum age for sub-aqua diving, but he didn't remember anything about ice skating.

"Tallulah's little sister goes with her and she's six, the same age as Matty," said Suze, coming to the rescue – or was she banging yet another nail into his coffin? There went using Matty as an excuse not to go.

"Don't you need your own skates?" he asked, helplessly clutching at straws. Even he remembered the old floppy hire skates that provided no support for the ankles. They were creased and worn, they smelled to high heaven, and he was sure you could catch verrucas from them too.

"Oh, Daddy," admonished Suze. "Everyone knows you can hire skates, but Tallulah has a spare pair if I want to borrow them."

"We can't all borrow them, though, can we?" he said, resigned.

And he made the necessary arrangements for the three of them to go on one of the public sessions as well as making an appointment to see an instructor afterwards.

The box office and foyer had changed a lot since he'd last been there. It was more like the swish entrances to some of the larger leisure complexes or even shopping centres. In his day it had just been a scruffy hatch in the wall, a dodgy looking plain-clothes door, and a single window display advertising a handful of skate-wear. Now there were food court booths, several boutiques, and a small amusement arcade. It didn't feel as seedy as it had the last time he'd been. They'd also sold half of the building to one of the big chain supermarkets, and they'd extended upwards to create a private fitness club. And it was much more illuminated and heated.

The biggest surprise were the hire skates. Gone were the old red (for girls and ladies) and black (for boys and men), worn leather floppy, scruffy skates. Instead they were of a much more rigid material, plastic almost, and in some of the brightest, fluorescent colours he'd ever seen. They could also choose between figure skates with the brake at the front, or hockey skates without.

Already, when he tied the laces that surprisingly didn't break, nor were they knotted where previously they had broken, his ankles felt much more supported. Gingerly, he got to his feet and, other than a bit of a wobble, he was able to walk to the gap in the perimeter without falling over.

"Hey!" he announced, quite proud of himself. "I can stand up."

Then he landed, with a bump, on the hard floor, on his bum, causing the girls to chortle with laughter.

Both Suze and Matty took walking in the skates in their stride. They watched from the seats for a few minutes before taking the leap. Dan tentatively stepped onto the ice first, immediately clinging to the side wall, and one-by-one helped his daughters do the same. A few desperate moves and they were standing up, if in a bendy kind of way, then the three of them took a few quick glidey moves.

Dan, as expected, was the first to land on the ice, but the girls thought it was hilariously funny and they all burst into more fits of laughter.

"Hey, Suze!" shouted a voice, and Suze's friend glided towards them looking very graceful. She had everything, all the gear, white figure skates, American tan thick denier tights, a fuchsia pink skating dress with a little jacket, and matching fluffy earmuffs and gloves. Her own little sister, dressed almost identically, but in acid orange, followed her.

"Hold our hands," Tallulah said.

"We'll take you around," said little Natasha.

"Can we, Dad?" asked Suze.

"Can we?" echoed her sister.

It sounded perfectly fine to him, and they'd never be far out of sight. Plus, it would give him chance to find his own ice legs without the embarrassment of his little girls watching him.

"Yay!" they cried, and off they went. Matty fell over almost immediately and Dan wanted to dash to her side. But she was soon up on her blades again, laughing, and off they went – again.

He clung to the side as he watched them complete a couple of circuits before bravely launching himself a few feet away, and he promptly lost his balance.

Dan's ankles were aching a bit with the unfamiliar strain. He'd not long recovered from a nasty fall on the snow in which he'd twisted one of his ankles. He flexed both feet a bit, bent down to tighten the laces, and tried again...

... and, actually, he managed a lot better than he thought he would. By the time he was able to carefully follow the four children, he was enjoying conquering the skates and wishing he'd pursued it when he was younger and more fearless than his sensible, adult self.

When it was time to take their skates back and meet the ice-skating instructor, the girls came back squealing with joy. Both Suze and Matty had taken to the ice like ducks to water – or penguins to ice – and their friends had even taught them a few easy dance steps.

Tallulah and Natasha swirled off in a flash of colour to join the others, spinning around the ice. Dan noticed that quite a lot of the children were wearing skating outfits, even some of the boys looking smart in their black trousers, white shirts and bow ties. Everyone else was either in tracksuits or regular jeans.

What looked like one of the coaches was headed in their direction.

"Do you want lessons or not?" he asked the girls, to another chorus of sing-song yeses. The attractive skating instructor smiled a beaming smile at them.

"Well?" she asked. "What did you think?"

"They really enjoyed themselves, thanks, and would love to have proper lessons."

"Really? That's great," she said, turning the smile on the girls.

"Er, do you teach adults too?" he spluttered out, surprising himself.

"Yes, we do," she said. And as she turned that stunning smile towards him he felt himself go slightly weak at the knees again, but this time it was nothing to do with the ice...

About the author

DIANE WORDSWORTH WAS born and bred in Solihull in the West Midlands when it was still Warwickshire. She started to write for magazines in 1985 and became a full-time freelance photojournalist in 1996. In 1998 she became sub-editor for several education trade magazines and started to edit classroom resources, textbooks and non-fiction books.

In 2004 Diane moved from the Midlands to South Yorkshire where she edited an in-house magazine for an international steel company for six years. She still edits and writes on a freelance basis.

Catch up with Diane today

Website: www.dianewordsworth.com[1]
Facebook page: www.facebook.com/DMWordsworth/[2]
Twitter: https://twitter.com/DMWordsworth
LinkedIn: www.linkedin.com/in/dianewordsworth[3]

---

1. http://www.dianewordsworth.com

2. http://www.facebook.com/DMWordsworth/

3. http://www.linkedin.com/in/dianewordsworth

Also by Diane Wordsworth

Marcie Craig mysteries
Night Crawler: a Marcie Craig Mystery

Toni & Bart time-travel tales
Mardi Gras: a Toni & Bart time-travel tale

Short Story Collections
Twee Tales
Twee Tales Too
Twee Tales Twee
Flash Fiction: five very short stories

Wordsworth Shorts
The Spirit of the Wind
The Most Scariest Night of the Year
The Girl on the Bench
Dancing on Ice
Happy Christmas, Santa
Careful What You Wish For
New Year's Revolution

One Born Every Minute
The Mystery of Woolley Dam
Martha's Favourite Doll
The Complete Angler

———— ⁙ ————

Short Tarot Tales
The Ace of Wands
The Ace of Cups

———— ⁙ ————

Writers' guides
Diary of a Scaredy Cat
Project Management for Writers: Gate 1

———— ⁙ ————

Other non-fiction
A History of Cadbury
The Life of Richard Cadbury

———— ⁙ ————

Magazine
Words Worth Writing

———— ⁙ ————

All available from
www.books2read.com/DianeWordsworth[1]

---

1. http://www.books2read.com/DianeWordsworth

Did you love *Twee Tales Too*? Then you should read *Twee Tales*² by Diane Wordsworth!

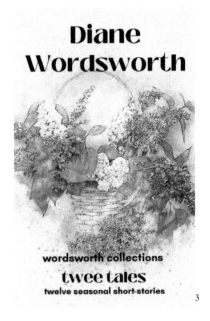

A collection of twelve short stories by Diane Wordsworth, three of which are totally brand new. The other nine have all been previously published in UK magazines or broadcast on BBC local radio.

This book was previously published as *Twee Tales* by Diane Parkin Read more at https://dianewordsworth.com.

2. https://books2read.com/u/4DE07k

3. https://books2read.com/u/4DE07k

About the Author

Diane Wordsworth was born and bred in Solihull in the West Midlands when it was still Warwickshire. She started to write for magazines in 1985 and became a full-time freelance photojournalist in 1996. In 1998 she became sub-editor for several education trade magazines and started to edit classroom resources, textbooks and non-fiction books.

In 2004 Diane moved from the Midlands to South Yorkshire where she edited an in-house magazine for an international steel company for six years. She still edits and writes on a freelance basis.

Read more at https://dianewordsworth.com.

Lightning Source UK Ltd.
Milton Keynes UK
UKHW020801230223
417513UK00014B/445